Kan

Also by Jamila Gavin

I WANT TO BE AN ANGEL
KAMLA AND KATE
THE SINGING BOWLS
THE WHEEL OF SURYA
THREE INDIAN PRINCESSES

Kamla and Kate Again

JAMILA GAVIN

Illustrated by Rhian Nest James

MAMMOTH

First published in Great Britain 1991
by Methuen Children's Books Ltd
Published 1992 by Mammoth
an imprint of Reed Consumer Books Ltd
Michelin House, 81 Fulham Road, London SW3 6RB
and Auckland, Melbourne, Singapore and Toronto

Text copyright © 1991 Jamila Gavin
Illustrations copyright © 1991 Rhian Nest James

The right of Jamila Gavin to be identified as author of
this work has been asserted by her in accordance with the
Copyright, Designs and Patents Act, 1988

ISBN 0 7497 1050 0

A CIP catalogue record for this title
is available from the British Library

Printed in Great Britain
by Cox & Wyman Ltd, Reading, Berkshire

This paperback is sold subject to the condition
that it shall not, by way of trade or otherwise,
be lent, resold, hired out, or otherwise circulated
without the publisher's prior consent in any form
of binding or cover other than that in which
it is published and without a similar condition
including this condition being imposed
on the subsequent purchaser.

Contents

1
A Topsy-Turvy Day

Kamla and Kate both liked being topsy-turvy. They liked to confuse everybody. Sometimes Kamla would call herself Kate, and Kate would call herself Kamla. They would do everything backwards. They would walk backwards and sometimes talk backwards and it was as though they had their own special language. Kamla became Almak, and Kate became Etak! So people were even more confused.

7

'Nac uoy yalp ta ym esuoh yadot? Kate asked Kamla.

'O sey, Etak! I nac!' replied Kamla enthusiastically.

Kate had thought that Kamla was very lucky being able to speak to her mother in Hindi, a language that not many other people knew where they lived. So she was very pleased when she and Kamla decided to invent their own backwards language which only the two of them knew.

When Kamla and Kate were being topsy-turvy, they would also say the opposite of what they meant. 'Today,' Kate would say to her mother, 'my nice is my nasty.'

'Oh I see,' laughed Mum. 'Today you will tell me you hate chocolate biscuits!'

'Yes!' agreed Kate.

'Oh well,' shrugged Mum. 'Then I'd better not buy any.'

'Mum!' exclaimed Kate, wondering if her mother was serious, or just joining in the game.

Things could go wrong when they played this game. Kamla was once walking backwards down the street, and bumped into a lamppost. It hurt a lot and made her eyes water.

'Serves you right,' said her mother severely. 'You should walk the right way round and look where you're going.'

Another time, the ice-cream van came jingling by. 'Who would like an ice cream?' shouted Kate's dad.

'Not me!' chorused the girls, wondering which flavour to choose. To their horror, the jingling didn't stop outside their house. 'Where are our ice creams?' they wailed.

'You said you didn't want one, so I didn't stop the van,' shrugged Dad.

'But we were only being topsy-turvy!' cried Kate.

'Well you should say what you mean,' replied Dad firmly.

Today was extra specially topsy-turvy. Kamla's and Kate's mothers had gone off on a day trip, so the two fathers had agreed to see to everything. When Kamla and Kate came walking backwards out of school, there were Kamla's dad and Kate's

dad waiting to meet them.

'Oh no!' groaned the two fathers when they saw their daughters. 'You're not being topsy-turvy today, are you?'

'Yes,' said Kate, 'and you must call me Kamla.'

'Yes,' said Kamla, 'and you must call me Kate.'

'I'll forget!' protested Kate's dad.

'I think we should only speak to them both at once and call them "You two",' suggested Kamla's dad.

'Definitely!' agreed Kate's dad. 'Come on, you two! Let's go home!'

When they were home, the girls went to play topsy-turvy games in the garden. They spoke to each other in their backwards language and called each other Almak and Etak. They swung upside down on the swing and only went down the slide backwards. The two dads went into the kitchen to prepare tea.

It seemed to take the dads a long time. Every now and then, the girls would call out, 'I hope tea's not ready yet, I'm so full up!'

Kate cried, 'I couldn't eat a thing.'

Kamla wailed, 'I feel as though my stomach will burst, I'm so full up!'

Of course they were being topsy-turvy, and what they really meant was, 'I'm starving, and I could eat a horse!'

At last the two dads called out, 'Hey, you two, tea's far from ready. There's no point in you coming. There's nothing to eat.'

For a split second, the two girls looked at each other in horror. 'Nothing to

eat? . . . But . . .' They began to exclaim. Then they burst out laughing. 'Oh it's our dads! They're just being topsy-turvy!'

They rushed indoors. Not through the door, but they dived headfirst through the open bay window, and landed with a plop on the sofa on the other side.

The two girls would like to have eaten their tea sitting under the table instead of at the table, but the two fathers said 'no'. So they gave in, and sat properly at the table, looking quite normal!

First Kamla's dad came in proudly carrying a plate full of steaming-hot samosas. 'Look what I've been making!' he said proudly.

'Ugh!' exclaimed Kamla, reaching out to grab one. 'I hate samosas!' And she stuffed it in her mouth.

'Really, Kamla!' frowned her father. 'Remember your manners. I know how much you like them, but I think you should have offered one to Kate first.'

But Kate looked at the *samosas* suspiciously. They looked nice. They smelt nice. But . . . Indian food often did

until you tasted it . . . and then . . . But . . .
she was so hungry she took one and
popped it into her mouth as Kamla had
done.

At first it tasted really good. She smiled
with pleasure and began to chew harder.

'It's delicious!' she cried. Then
suddenly, she gave a screech, 'Aaaah!' and
leapt from the table. She clasped her hand
to her mouth. Her face went red, and
tears streamed down her cheeks. She ran
round in circles. 'Water, water!' she
gasped.

Kamla thrust a glass of orange juice into
her hand. Kate gulped it down. She stuck
out her tongue as if it were on fire and
panted, 'What burnt my mouth?'

'Oh dear!' Kamla's dad gave an
apologetic sigh. 'I must have put in too
much chilli.'

'Chilli?' exclaimed Kate. 'But this was
hot, hot, hot! Not chilly!'

Kamla burst out laughing. 'Oh, Kate!'
she chortled. 'That's really topsy-turvy.
You see, Indian chillis are hot not chilly!
I'll show you one.' She jumped from the

table and ran to the kitchen. She came back bearing a small, dark green pod on the palm of her hand. It looked as cool as a pea pod.

'Did a little thing like that set my whole mouth on fire?' asked Kate.

'I'm afraid it did,' said Kamla's dad. 'Nature can be very topsy-turvy too.'

Then Kate's dad came in next. Up high he carried a plate with a cake on it. 'This is

15

my offering!' he said, solemnly setting it down in the middle of the table.

'What's that?' asked Kate with a puzzled look.

'Is it a special kind of pudding?' asked Kamla politely.

'No it is *not*!' pouted Kate's dad. 'It's a cake. Can't you tell?'

'It seems rather thin for a cake,' murmured Kate.

'More like a big biscuit,' thought Kamla.

'Oh dear!' sighed Kate's dad. 'I did use self-raising flour, but instead of rising up it sank into the middle.'

'I think our tea has turned out a bit of a muddle,' said Kamla's dad.

'A bit topsy-turvy, if you ask me,' agreed Kate's dad.

'Just like us!' cried the girls.

'Come on you two!' shouted the two dads after a whispered conference between them. 'We're all going down to have tea, toast and buns at the tea shop, and if you're not too topsy-turvy, we might treat you to an ice cream.'

'Oh pooh!' beamed the two girls,

leaping to their feet enthusiastically. 'We hate ice cream!'

That night, when the two mothers got home, each went to her daughter's bedroom to say good night. Each found her daughter sleeping the wrong way round, with her head at the foot of the bed and her toes at the head.

'Am I supposed to say good night to your toes?' grinned Kate's mother.

'Are your feet interested in a bedtime story?' asked Kate's mother.

The two girls smiled sleepily. 'Mum,' each said, 'we've had a topsy-turvy day all day today, so we thought we might as well go to sleep topsy-turvy. But tomorrow, I think we'll just stay the right way round.'

'Oh good,' said the mums. 'I think it makes life easier.' Then they each kissed their daughter's toes and went downstairs.

2

Kate Wants a Skateboard

Kamla and Kate were on their way to the park.

Suddenly there was a rumbling and mumbling, a clattering and rattling, a thuddering and juddering. They jumped aside, as a cluster of skateboarders came zooming along the pavement.

How free they looked! How happy they looked!

'It must be as good as flying!' exclaimed Kate. 'I wish I had a skateboard!'

The skateboarders swept past, their arms outstretched like tightrope walkers to balance themselves; some wore helmets and pads to protect their heads, elbows and knees.

'It must hurt when you fall,' murmured Kamla.

When the girls arrived at the park, the skateboarders were whirling about on the paved area around the water fountain. They did zigzags and flips and twists and jumps, and such daring tricks like bouncing themselves on the sides of the fountain, that Kamla was sure someone would get hurt in the end. But no one did. Not that day, anyway.

'Oh I DO wish I had a skateboard,' repeated Kate.

'I'd rather have roller skates,' said Kamla.

A boy on a skateboard hurtled unsteadily towards them.

'I know him!' cried Kamla. 'That's Sanjay!'

Sanjay wore the helmet, the knee pads, the elbow pads, and he had on a pair of brand new trainers. But all his flashy new gear couldn't disguise the fact that Sanjay hadn't been skateboarding very long, and though he stretched his arms out to balance himself, his head stuck out forwards and his bottom stuck out backwards, and he looked very wobbly indeed.

'Look out!' yelled Kamla as he rushed straight at them. But just as they were about to dodge out of his way, Sanjay jumped off his skateboard and let it run harmlessly on to the grass.

'Hiya, Kamla! Hiya, Kate!' he called out cheerfully. 'I got all this for my birthday!'

'So I see,' said Kamla tartly.

'You lucky thing!' sighed Kate enviously. 'I think I'll ask for a skateboard for my birthday, but it's ages away yet!'

'Shall I show you some new tricks? I've been practising!' cried Sanjay.

'Sanjay's an awful show-off,' whispered Kamla with a grin.

'Can you do jumps?' asked Kate.

'Sure I can,' boasted Sanjay. 'Watch me!' He scooted off down the path and

began to attempt little jumps and flips. He looked very wobbly, and kept tumbling off. Kamla and Kate pretended not to notice.

After a while he came rumbling back, standing more upright this time, hoping to look like a champion. He tried to do a racing stop right in front of them, but he fell off. 'I nearly did it!' he said.

'Please can I have a go?' begged Kate.

Sanjay looked reluctant. 'Well . . .'

'Please!' Kate implored him. 'Just a little go.'

'Let her have a go, Sanjay!' cried Kamla. 'She's ever so good at that sort of thing.'

'Oh, all right, but just a little go. I want to practise,' growled Sanjay, and he pushed the skateboard over to Kate. 'It's brand new, you know, so don't let it bash into anything and get scratched!' he warned.

Kate went over to the skateboard. It was like a huge flat roller skate. First she put one foot on it and rolled it up and down. Then taking Kamla's hand, she stood on it with both feet to get the feel of it.

'You have to scoot along for a bit, then jump on!' instructed Sanjay.

Still clutching Kamla's hand, Kate began to scoot along. As they got faster,

Kamla began to run. 'Jump on, jump on!' she squealed.

Kate put both feet on to the skateboard. 'Look at me!' she shrieked with glee. Then she began to sway about dangerously. 'Oh, oh, oh!' she cried, and leapt off.

The skateboard went rolling away. Kamla raced after it. It was was heading for the litter bin. Sanjay hid his eyes with a groan, but Kamla caught it just in time, and held it up above her head. 'See! Not a mark on it! Can I have a go now, Sanjay?'

'Must you?' frowned Sanjay.

'Please!' begged Kamla.

'Hurry up then,' muttered Sanjay, 'or I won't get any time on it myself.'

Kamla scooted along, and Kate ran alongside her holding her hand. The skateboard was running smoothly. She was doing quite well. Kamla jumped on with both feet.

'It's great!' shrieked Kamla.

Then they came to a slight slope. The skateboard went faster. Kate couldn't keep up and let go of Kamla's hand.

Kamla immediately began to wobble and sway.

'Help!' she wailed, and fell off, rolling on to her knees.

The skateboard raced away. Kate didn't know what to do: rush over to help Kamla, or try and stop the skateboard from crashing into the wall.

'Oh no!' yelled Sanjay. 'My beautiful new skateboard! Save it, save it!'

At that moment, walking down the path, came Sanjay's older sister, Muni. How grown-up she looked in her flowing, elegant saree, with her hair tightly plaited into one long plait, which dangled down her back, and her arms tinkling with bangles.

She swooped down and caught the runaway skateboard, while Kate rushed over to Kamla who was bent over, clutching her knees.

'I knew it would hurt,' Kamla winced, fighting back the tears.

'They're not bleeding,' said Kate comfortingly, examining her knees.

'Obviously, skateboarding is too hard

24

for you,' commented Sanjay, striding over.

'No, it's not,' retorted Kate. 'We just need practice.'

'Well, you're not practising on mine.' He held out his hands to take the skateboard from Muni.

But Muni didn't hand it back. She held it lovingly in her arms with a strange look in her eye. She looked around as if to check whether anyone was watching, then she said, 'Sanjay, just let me have a little go. I promise not to crash it.'

'You?' exclaimed Sanjay staring at his sister in amazement.

'You?' chorused Kamla and Kate looking up at her, wide-eyed.

'You can't skateboard in a saree!' cried Kate.

'I can do anything in a saree,' laughed Muni. 'Well, almost anything!'

Then Sanjay remembered. Only a year ago, before Muni took to wearing sarees and being grown-up, she had been such a tomboy. You hardly ever saw her out of jeans: climbing, biking, roller-skating, and rough and tumbling with the best of them. There was nothing Muni wouldn't do, or at least try to do. She was the bravest of brave. But that was last year. This year, she had turned seventeen, got a job and was now nearly engaged to be married. How could she even think of going skateboarding?

'Please, Sanjay?' She tipped her head on one side and gave him a pleading smile.

'Go on then,' said her brother, gruffly. 'I just hope no one sees you. What would Dad say? What would Naresh say?' Naresh was the young man people said Muni was going to marry.

Muni didn't seem to care. She hoisted up her saree with one hand, and began to scoot off down the path. She went faster and faster, then jumped on with both feet. Her saree billowed out behind her, and she looked like a beautiful sailing boat racing in the wind.

'Look at her!' breathed Kate admiringly. 'She's good!'

'She's the best in the world,' sighed Kamla.

26

'I'm nearly as good as that,' said Sanjay. 'Oh, no! Look who's coming!'

Kamla and Kate turned to see. They all groaned. 'Oh, no!' Walking smartly towards them, with his black hair sleeked back, wearing his dark, grey, city suit, was Naresh.

'Muni, Muni!' The girls began to run. 'Stop, Muni! Look who's here.'

Muni heard their voices. She turned, lost her balance and began to wave her arms about as she tried to recover herself. But it was no good. The skateboard sped towards the grass, struck soft earth and tipped Muni headlong into the flowerbeds.

Kamla and Kate raced towards her. Hastily, they helped her to her feet. She looked very crumpled. Kamla tried to smooth down Muni's saree, and Kate brushed off the bits of earth and twigs which were clinging to her back, and all the time they whispered, 'Naresh is here! Naresh is here!'

'So what!' cried Muni defiantly. 'I haven't broken the law.'

Naresh came up and stood, frowning. 'Have you forgotten we're visiting the Anands this afternoon?'

'No, Naresh! I hadn't forgotten.' Then she re-wound part of her saree, flicked off some twigs, pushed some loose hair behind her ears and smiled sweetly. 'I was only having a go on Sanjay's skateboard while waiting for you. Where have you been? You're late!'

Naresh stopped frowning and grinned. 'Oh come on, you! Leave skateboarding to the kids. You're supposed to be a lady now,' and he took her arm gently and led her away.

'Well I'm off too,' cried Sanjay. He snatched up his skateboard as if afraid someone else would come along and ask for a go, and pushed off as fast as he could.

'I wish I had a skateboard,' repeated Kate.

'I don't,' said Kamla, ruefully examining her grazed knees. 'I think I'll stick to roller-skating. I'm better at that.'

Some weeks later, there was a knock on Kate's door. There on the doorstep were Kamla, Sanjay and Muni. Kamla was carrying the skateboard, Muni was carrying his helmet and pads and Sanjay had an arm up to the elbow in plaster.

Muni suggested she talk to Kate's mum and dad alone. Kamla and Sanjay were very secretive, and wouldn't tell Kate why they had come.

'What did you do to your arm?' asked Kate.

'I broke it falling off my skateboard,' muttered Sanjay.

'He doesn't want to go skateboarding ever again,' announced Kamla. 'Isn't that lucky?'

Kate didn't know why that was lucky until her mother, father and Muni reappeared. Her father was carrying the skateboard and her mother was carrying the helmet and pads.

'Sanjay doesn't want his skateboard any more,' said Muni. 'So we decided to sell it to you. Unless you're afraid of breaking your arm too!'

'Oh, I'm not afraid!' exclaimed Kate, her eyes shining with joy.

'But remember,' said Mum, 'it's an early birthday present.'

'A very early birthday present,' agreed

Dad, and he put the skateboard into Kate's arms.

Kate could hardly speak, she was so excited. As Muni left, she bent down and whispered in Kate's ear, 'You will let me have a go sometimes, won't you?'

'Oh yes!' nodded Kate, 'any time you like!'

3

The School-bag

'What have you got in your bag?' asked Kate curiously.

The new boy stood in the cloakroom at school. He was new all over. New anorak, new trousers, shining new shoes and a brand new school-bag.

Their teacher, Mrs Bray, had asked Kamla and Kate to look after the new boy. They had to show him his peg in the cloakroom, then take him down the corridor to their classroom.

His name was Kevin, so they took him to the peg with a new label with his name on it, next to other names beginning with K, such as Kiram, Kirsty, Kamla and Kate.

Kevin hung up his anorak and hung up his scarf, but he didn't hang up his school-bag.

'What have you got in your bag?' asked Kamla. 'Is it precious?'

Kevin lowered his eyes to the ground and wouldn't speak, but clutched his bag tightly to his chest and would not hang it up on the peg.

'We're not supposed to take our school-bags into the classroom,' Kate told him.

'Mrs Bray will take it away from you,' added Kamla. 'You're supposed to hang it up on the peg with your jacket.'

But Kevin would not let go of his bag.

Kamla and Kate took Kevin along to the classroom. They told their teacher that Kevin wouldn't hang up his bag. Mrs Bray came over to him and spoke gently.

'Kevin, dear! Let me hang up your bag on the peg. It will be quite safe. You can

have it at break-time. If everyone brought
their school-bags into the classroom, we'd
always be tripping up over them, because
there's no room.'

But Kevin fiercely held his bag to his
chest and would not let go.

'Oh well,' smiled Mrs Bray patiently.
'Because you are new, I'll let you keep it

with you till you feel safer with us, but try not to let it get in the way.'

'What has he got in his bag?' the other children whispered to Kamla and Kate.

But they shrugged. 'We don't know. He won't tell us.'

When break-time came, some of the children rushed to the cloakroom and opened up their bags. They had brought toys to play with in the playground. Some had brought dinky cars, motorbikes, skipping ropes and marbles; some had brought little ponies with manes that needed brushing, dolls that needed dressing, or green, fluffy spiders which hung on the end of string to dangle in front of people and make them scream.

Kamla and Kate looked at Kevin. What would he take out of his bag?

But Kevin didn't open his bag. He just went out into the playground and held it tightly to his chest. He wouldn't tell anybody what was inside. He wouldn't play ball, he wouldn't play tag and he wouldn't even play kiss chase! All he did was stand in a corner holding his bag.

When lunch-time came, some children took their packed lunches out of their school-bags. But Kevin hadn't brought a packed lunch. He was going to eat a school lunch. He stood in line, clutching a tray and took a steaming hot meal to sit at a table and eat it with a knife and fork, and still he would not let go of his bag.

After lunch Kate said to Kevin, 'Can we guess what is inside your bag?' And Kamla said, 'If we guess right, will you show us?' Kevin just shrugged.

'Is it your favourite teddy?' asked Kate.

'No.'

'Is it a special car?' asked Kamla.

'No.'

'Is it a purse full of money?'

'No.'

'Is it a deadly snake, or a spider, or a bug in a box?'

'No.' Kevin shook his head and almost smiled.

'I think it's empty. I don't think you've got anything in there at all,' said Kamla.

'I have!' burst out Kevin.

But Kamla and Kate got bored with

asking and went off to play.

That day in school was 'showing day'. It was a day when children could bring something to school which they thought was interesting, and show it to everybody.

That afternoon, after lunch, the children put away their toys and took out of their bags the things they had brought to show.

'Right!' said Mrs Bray, when the children had all settled at their tables. 'Who has brought something in for all of us to see?'

A flurry of hands went up. Mrs Bray looked very pleased. 'All right, Tom! You come first,' she said to Tom Clay.

Tom came to the front of the class and held up a bird's nest for all to see.

'I found it on my way to school. It was empty,' he added.

'Good,' said Mrs Bray, 'because no one should steal a bird's eggs, and no one should take away a bird's nest in the nesting season.' Everyone admired the nest, and noticed that it wasn't just made of twigs, but also of bits of paper, ribbons, fur and human hair! All had been moulded and woven together to make the perfect nest.

Then Lisa Porter came up. She showed the class a bit of shrapnel. It was an ugly piece of metal; hard and sharp and looking as though it wanted to hurt.

'My granddad dug it up in the garden,' she told them. 'He recognised it

38

immediately, because he was a soldier in the war.'

Kiram Aziz stood up next. His uncle had just returned from Pakistan. Look what he brought back! Kiram held up a wriggly snake! Everybody shuddered and squealed. Then they saw that it was only made of wood.

'Isn't it beautiful!' exclaimed Mrs Bray. 'It's made from so many pieces of wood, held together by shiny silver nails, that it almost looks alive!'

One by one, the children came up. Kate showed a fossil, Kamla showed her glass bangles, and almost everyone showed something. Only Kevin sat there, clutching his school-bag. Only he looked as if he would not show them anything.

'Well!' smiled Mrs Bray. 'It looks as though that's everyone.' She didn't look at Kevin. She didn't want him to feel bad. 'Thank you all for showing us your interesting things.'

Then suddenly a small voice said, 'I've got something to show.'

Everyone looked at Kevin. He still sat

with his school-bag on his knee, but this time he wasn't holding it quite so tightly.

'Do you have something to show us, Kevin?' asked Mrs Bray, kindly.

Kevin nodded, and slowly walked up to the top of the class. Everyone leaned forward. Everyone's eyes were staring hard as he opened up his school-bag. Everyone held their breath, as Kevin put his hand inside the bag. What would it be? Kevin held it up. Everyone groaned with disappointment.

'It's nothing but an egg cup!' someone cried.

Mrs Bray frowned and looked at the egg cup which Kevin was holding. 'It's a very pretty egg cup,' she said, trying to find something nice to say.

'Mine's much nicer!' muttered another. 'So's mine,' said a third.

'Just a moment, just a moment!' Mrs Bray tried to calm down the indignant voices. 'Let's see what Kevin has to say about it.'

'My egg cup is wooden,' whispered Kevin. 'It's painted yellow and red, and it's . . . it's . . .' he paused. 'It's magic!' he said, spreading out his hands.

Magic? The word hung in the air. All the children leaned forwards again, their eyes wide with expectation. 'How magic? Show us!' They said.

Kevin held the egg cup in front of him. He shook it, and showed everyone that it was empty. Then he suddenly pressed it upside down on to the palm of his hand. He closed his eyes and said in a loud voice, 'Abracadabra, of this I beg! Fill my cup with a nice brown egg!' Then Kevin turned up the cup and looked inside. With a great smile of triumph, he tipped the cup again, and a brown wooden egg rolled out on to the palm of his hand.

'Wow!' the class gasped with amazement. 'That's brilliant!' they exclaimed.

'How did you do it?' cried Kamla.

'Show us again!' urged Kate.

Kevin put the egg back in the egg cup. He tipped it over on to the palm of his hand; said the magic words, 'Abracadabra, of this I beg! Take away my

nice brown egg!'

He held the egg cup up. It was empty. The egg had gone.

'Do it again!' the children implored him. So Kevin did it again and again, but no one could guess how he did it.

'I told you it was magic!' smiled Kevin mysteriously.

'Now I know why you wouldn't let go of your bag,' laughed Kamla.

'I wish you'd teach me some tricks,' sighed Kate. 'I've always wanted to be a magician.'

By the end of the afternoon, Kevin didn't feel quite so new any more. Everyone wanted to be his friend, and the next day when he came to school, he went over to the pegs where the Ks were: Kirsty, Kiram, Kamla, Kate and Kevin. He hung up his anorak, he hung up his scarf and he also hung up his new school-bag.

4
When Upside Down is Best

'What are you doing?' Kate asked Kamla.

'I'm thinking,' said Kamla.

'What are you thinking about?' asked Kate curiously, because Kamla was just sitting there staring into space.

'I'm not thinking about anything,' replied Kamla. 'I'm just thinking.'

'You must be thinking about something if you're thinking,' insisted Kate.

'Why must I?' murmured Kamla.

'Otherwise you wouldn't be thinking,' grumbled Kate. 'Anyway, I'm thinking too, and I'm thinking proper thoughts.'

'Oh?' exclaimed Kamla. Now she looked interested. 'Like what?'

'I'm thinking that I'm bored, and I wish you'd stop thinking about nothing and help me think about something, like what we can do!'

'Hmm . . .' grunted Kamla. 'Let me think . . .'

'Shall we play ponies?' suggested Kate.

'No, we played that yesterday,' said Kamla shaking her head.

'Hospitals?' Kate tried again. 'I could pretend to fall and break my leg, and you could . . .'

'You're always the patient,' complained Kamla. 'Never me. I don't want to play hospitals. We're always playing hospitals.'

Just then, it started raining, so they had to stop talking and run inside squealing.

'Shh!' Kamla's mother put a finger to her lips. 'Chachaji is meditating, and mustn't be disturbed.'

'What's Chachaji?' asked Kate. 'It sounds like a chuff-chuff train!'

'That's what I call my grandfather!'

45

laughed Kamla. 'Just you wait till I tell him you thought he was a train!'

'Kamla's grandfather has just arrived to stay with us for a few days,' explained Kamla's mother. 'He's a little tired after his journey, and he needs a bit of peace and quiet so that he can meditate.'

'What's meditating?' asked Kate.

'I don't really know,' shrugged Kamla, 'but my grandfather's always doing it.' She looked around to see if anyone was watching, but her mother had disappeared into the kitchen. 'Chachaji's in the living room, shall we peep in and see?'

Kate nodded, full of curiosity. The two girls crept to the living-room door. It was firmly shut. They listened, but not a sound came from inside. Kamla put a finger to her lips, then ever so slowly and carefully, she turned the door knob. The door opened silently. Kamla peered inside. Then she beckoned Kate to have a look. Kate peered inside. She drew back, astonished. 'Is that meditating?' she whispered. 'It looks topsy-turvy to me!'

46

'Why don't you come in!' said an old, kind, quiet voice. Kamla and Kate looked at each other, amazed. They had been so silent. How did he know they were there? Kamla pushed the door wide open, and the two girls shyly came into the room.

There in the middle of the carpet was Kamla's grandfather, standing on his head.

He looked up at them from upside down and smiled. 'Hello, Kamla! Is this your friend, Kate?'

'Yes, Chachaji, this is Kate.'

'How do you do, Kate!' And even though he was balanced on his head upside down, he stretched out a hand for her to shake.

Kate bent down and took his hand. 'How do you do!' she said.

'Forgive me for staying upside down,' said the old man. 'I had a rather tiring journey, and my brain needs refreshment.'

'Oh,' said Kate, in an understanding voice. 'That's all right. I like being topsy-turvy too sometimes.'

'It helps to get the blood to the brain,' explained grandfather. 'And that is a good thing. It improves your memory and helps you to learn better. Do you find that?' he enquired.

'I don't know. I've never thought about it. When I do cartwheels and handstands I sometimes feel dizzy, but I've never stood on my head.'

'Then you must try it, my dear,' murmured the old man, and he closed his eyes.

The two girls crept from the room. 'Does he go to sleep upside down as well?' asked Kate.

'Of course not,' laughed Kamla. 'He just sometimes closes his eyes to help him concentrate.'

'I know what we can do today!' cried Kate. 'Let's try and meditate too!'

Kamla thought this was a very good idea. So they went up to Kamla's bedroom and cleared a space in the middle. Then they bent down, put their heads to the floor and tried to push up and get their legs into the air.

It wasn't as easy as grandfather made it look. Kate wobbled about and kept toppling over, and Kamla simply couldn't get her feet off the ground.

'Meditating's quite hard!' they gasped.

'It's only hard upside down,' said Kamla. 'I don't think you have to be upside down to meditate.'

'Oh?' said Kate, still puzzled. 'How else can you meditate?'

'My dad says he meditates in the bath,' said Kamla, 'and my mum says she meditates while she's peeling the potatoes.'

'I see,' said Kate earnestly, though she didn't really.

'Let's bend over and try again. Chachaji says it helps you to learn, and I need to learn my eight times table by tomorrow.'

'Oh yes! So do I!' cried Kate. They both immediately bent over and put their heads to the ground.

It was so quiet in the house that Kamla's mother wondered what was going on. She went upstairs to investigate. She found Kamla and Kate bent over on all fours with their heads on the ground and their bottoms in the air. 'What are you playing?' she asked.

'We're not playing, we're meditating and trying to learn our eight times table,' said Kamla.

'Do you know your eight times table?' asked Kamla's mother.

'No,' said Kate. But we thought if we stood on our heads, we would get to know it.'

'I'm afraid it's not as simple as that. Someone has to teach it to you first, then standing on your heads might help you to remember it. Shall I help?' asked Kamla's mum, nicely.

The two girls flopped back on their heels. 'Yes please,' they said.

For an hour, Mum taught the girls their eight times table. Then at last it was time for Kate to go home.

That night, when Kate's mother came up to kiss her daughter good night, she found Kate standing on her head. 'What on earth are you doing?' she asked.

'I'm learning my eight times table, by meditating,' said Kate.

'Good heavens!' exclaimed Mum. 'I didn't know you could meditate.'

'Kamla's grandfather meditates standing on his head,' said Kate.

'I suppose everyone has their own method,' smiled Mum. 'I meditate when I walk the dog.'

As Mum tucked Kate into bed, Kate said, 'I'm still not really sure what meditating is. I know you can meditate in the bath or walking the dog or standing on your head, but what is it?'

'Meditating means to think seriously and deeply about something,' said Mum.

'Oh,' whispered Kate, as she fell asleep.

'I do that all the time.'

The next day at school, Kamla and Kate had to say their eight times table to their teacher. They knew it perfectly. 'You did learn that quickly!' exclaimed Mrs Bray. 'How did you do it?'

'We learnt it standing on our heads,' said the girls. 'Shall we show you?'

'No, no!' laughed their teacher, otherwise everyone will want to learn their lessons upside down!'

After school, Kamla came to play at Kate's house. Kate just sat silently on the swing, staring into space.

'What are you doing?' asked Kamla.

'I'm meditating,' replied Kate.

'What are you meditating about?' asked Kamla.

'About what we should play,' answered Kate.

'Oh,' murmured Kamla. 'Perhaps we should stand on our heads.'

'I think it's easier on the swing,' answered Kate dreamily.

'Mmm,' sighed Kamla and climbed on to the other swing. For a while they swung to and fro in silent meditation, then Kate said, 'Shall we play hospitals?'

'Oh yes,' agreed Kamla, 'and this time, you be the doctor and I'll be the patient.'

'All right,' nodded Kate, 'but let's meditate a little longer. It's nice on the swing.'

5

Going for Gold

Kamla and Kate were up to something. They seemed to spend a lot of time doing unusual things, like hopping round the garden on one leg or racing up and down with their skipping ropes. Once Kamla's grandfather caught them pinching two eggs from the fridge and two spoons from the kitchen drawer. 'Now what are you up to?' he demanded.

'Nothing,' sang Kamla innocently. 'It's just a game.'

Grandfather shrugged and let them go. He watched them curiously out of the window and wondered what kind of game it was. When they dropped their eggs with a split and a splat, he wouldn't let them have any more. 'It's wrong to waste food,' he said sternly, 'when half the world is starving.' So they used potatoes instead.

And when that game was over, they stood side by side and tied their inside legs together. When they tried to run up the garden, all they did was stumble and fall in a giggling heap. 'What strange games children play these days,' thought Grandfather.

Then one Friday morning, everyone seemed to be extra specially interested in the weather. The first thing Kamla did when she woke up was to look out of the window and up at the sky. 'Oh no!' she moaned. 'It looks like rain.'

Her mother looked out and stared at the tumbling grey clouds. 'I wonder what the weather forecast is?' she murmured.

'It doesn't look too good at all,' muttered her dad.

Grandfather went outside. He stood on one leg with his arms upstretched and his face turned to the heavens. After a minute, he came back indoors and said, 'It won't rain today. I can feel it in my bones.'

The first thing Kate did when she woke up was to look out of the window. 'Oh, Mum!' she wailed. 'Do you think it's going to rain? If it does it will ruin everything.'

Mum looked out the window. 'There seems to be a wind, and the clouds are on the move,' she said encouragingly.

'The weather forecast says, "brightening later"' Dad informed them from in front of early morning television.

'It's got to stay dry, it's just got to stay dry,' muttered Kate fiercely.

When Kamla and Kate arrived in school, all the teachers were looking out of the windows as well.

'I hope it doesn't rain and make all my white lines go funny,' said Mr Hicks.

'I hope it doesn't rain on all the chairs I've put out,' said Miss Jones.

'I hope it doesn't rain and ruin all the flags I've draped round the railings,' said Miss Lal.

'I just hope we don't have to cancel,' murmured the head teacher with a worried look.

'My grandfather says it won't rain,' announced Kamla.

'How does he know?' everyone asked.

'Because he felt it in his bones,' she said.

The children tried to concentrate on their reading, but they couldn't help glancing out the window. They could see the grey clouds hanging over them, threatening to burst with torrents of rain.

But by break-time, the clouds didn't seem to be so low, and some children shouted, 'Look! Little blue patches!'

By lunch-time, the blue patches had got bigger and bigger, so they looked like lakes up in the sky, and the clouds looked like islands floating by. And bursting through, making everyone cheer for joy, was a great yellow sun pouring down sunbeams.

'Your grandfather was right!' cried Kate excitedly.

'Come on, children!' called Mr Hicks. 'You can all change into your shorts and T-shirts, and put on your trainers.'

At home, Kate's mother changed into a nice, summery, flowery dress. Kate's dad said he would wear his new Panama straw hat!

Kamla's mum put on her light, pink saree, and her dad wore a smart pair of beige cotton trousers. 'But I'll take the umbrella too, just in case!' he said.

'What's all this dressing up in aid of?' asked Grandfather.

'We've got to go to Kamla's school! Today's the big day!'

'What big day?' asked Grandfather. But

nobody answered him because they were too busy rushing. So Grandfather put on his crisply starched Indian trousers, and stood by the front door, ready to go.

When they got to school, the playing fields were already swirling with people. Mums and dads, toddlers and babies, aunts and grandparents all paraded around while the excitement built up. Then a voice boomed an announcement through the loudspeaker.

'Ladies and gentlemen! Please take your places. The events are about to begin.'

'What is happening?' asked Grandfather, bewildered.

'Come on!' cried Kamla's mother, grabbing his arm. 'We mustn't miss Kamla and Kate in the egg and spoon.'

Kamla's mum, dad and grandfather all gathered by the running track. Kate's mum and dad joined them and they chatted excitedly. The children appeared and lined up at the top of the field. Each child held a spoon containing a hard-boiled egg which wouldn't go 'splat' if it dropped.

'Ah ha!' exclaimed Grandfather, remembering the game. 'So that's what they've been up to.' He looked at Kamla and Kate. They stood with one foot forward on the starting line; their faces were tense, their eyes fixed on the finishing tape.

'Ready, steady, go!' yelled Mr Hicks. As the children set off, Grandfather began to dance up and down with excitement. 'Come on, Kamla! Come on, Kate!' Some children had started running, desperate to get there first. But that was a mistake; the eggs fell from their spoons and they were out of the race.

Others went along too slowly, their arms outstretched, and their eyes glued to the egg as if their stare would hold it to the spoon. They soon got left behind.

Kamla and Kate were doing quite well. They had been practising really hard. They went at a fast, smooth, steady walk. They each thought that they could get there first, but, oh no! Who was coming up from behind to overtake? It was Darren Thompson, walking so fast he was almost running.

'Come on, Kate! Come on, Darren! Come on, Kamla!' Voices rang out from all sides. Darren drew level with Kamla. Kamla looked at him. Oh no! That was fatal. Her walk wobbled, her hand shook and her egg rolled off the spoon. Kamla was out. Now Darren was catching up with Kate.

'Come on Kate! Come on Darren!' How the voices were yelling furiously. They were neck and neck now. The markers at the finishing tape leaned forward to see who was going to cross the tape first.

Kamla and Darren both strode through. It looked as though they had both won. But the markers said no. Darren's arm was a little longer than Kate's so he had just got over the finishing line first. Darren was first. Kate was second. Kamla rushed over and hugged her. 'I thought you were first!' she cried.

When they weren't racing, Kamla and Kate sat with their class watching and cheering on the other races. Their next race was the three-legged race.

'Oooh!' said Kamla with a shiver. 'I'm nervous.'

'Oooh!' agreed Kate. 'I'm nervous too. I just hope we don't fall.'

'We must make sure we start with our outside leg,' cautioned Kamla.

At last the three-legged race was announced through the loudspeaker. Kamla and Kate leapt up all of a jitter and ran over to the starting line. Mr Hicks tied their inside legs together and they clasped their arms around each other's waist. Then they stood in line.

'Ready, steady, go!' yelled Mr Hicks.

Kamla and Kate waited just that half second to make sure they both started off on the outside leg. Then they were off. Already some were tumbling down, because one had started on a different leg to the other.

'One, two, one, two,' whispered Kate as they sped along with a swinging rhythm which kept them together.

'Come on, Kamla! Come on, Kate!' The voices were cheering louder and louder as they raced past their class. In front of them were Sharon and Maya, coming up behind them were Jason and Ben. Faster! Faster! Kate increased the rhythm. Now they were neck and neck with Sharon and Katy, now they were overtaking!

'Yes, yes, yes!' yelled Kamla's and Kate's friends and parents.

'Go for gold!' yelled Kate's dad.

'Yahoo!' yelled Kamla's grandfather, as Kamla and Kate raced over the finishing line first.

'We did it!' screamed Kamla and Kate, and tumbled to the ground in an exhausted heap.

After that, Kate came third in the skipping race and Kamla came second in the hopping race, but the best was still to come. Suddenly, the loudspeaker announced the Mothers' race.

There was a buzz of curiosity. Children craned their necks round trying to see if their mothers would take part.

'Oh no!' exclaimed Kate with a giggle. 'My mum's got up! She can't run for monkey nuts!'

'My mum's got up too!' cried Kamla.

'But your mum's wearing a saree,' said Kate. 'How can she possibly run a race?'

'You'll see!' laughed Kamla. 'She can run like the wind.'

Lots of brave mothers had now lined up. They kicked off their shoes. 'Anything for a laugh!' someone said.

'On your marks!' yelled Mr Hicks. The mothers stopped chatting. They each put their best foot forward on to the starting line. 'Get set!' They braced themselves. 'Go!' They were off.

There were all sorts of mothers racing down the track. Nice round cuddly ones, who trundled along as fast as they could; young, tough, lean-looking mums, who wore jeans and shirts and galloped along and neat, slim elegant mums who couldn't run very fast because their skirts were too tight. Kate's mother ran with her flowery dress billowing and Kamla's mum ran in her pink, flowing, cotton saree which she had hauled up with one hand.

At first, Kamla's mum looked as though she would be last. She started slowly and was lagging behind. But suddenly, when she was halfway down the field, she found her stride, and soon she overtook them all.

Kamla and Kate were jumping up and down cheering her on. Kamla was right. Her mother ran like the wind, and she just flew over the finishing line, easily the first.

'Oh look at my poor mum!' chuckled Kate. Her mother, smiling broadly, waved merrily to them as she crossed the finishing line last. She didn't mind. It was just fun to take part.

Grandfather stood on one leg and

stretched his arms up to the skies. 'My
bones tell me it's going to rain,' he
murmured.

'It mustn't rain before they hand out the prizes!' cried Kate.

A lady mayoress in her gold chain had come for the sports day, and was waiting to hand out the prizes and silver cups. She made a very long speech, and people groaned, as the grey clouds piled up overhead.

Kamla and Kate went up together to receive a little silver cup for winning the three-legged race.

Kamla's mother got a pot of flowers for winning the Mothers' race.

'Come on now!' urged Kate's father. 'There's one more race to be run. Let's see if we can run home before it rains.'

As everybody scattered and hurried away, and umbrellas opened and plastic macs unfolded, the rain came down. It made all the white lines of the racing track go funny, it rained on the empty chairs and it soaked all the flags hanging round the railings and made them soggy.

But nobody cared. Sports day was over, and everyone had had a wonderful afternoon.

6

What Can we do Today?

Whenever Granny came to stay, Kate had to be on her best behaviour, otherwise she would have a saying quoted at her like 'Waste not want not'. But Kate still liked Granny. She did all the good things grannies do, such as give her sweets, slip her the odd fifty pence, help her with a jigsaw or play snap with her.

Granny was staying for a few days. She and Kate had just eaten lunch while Kate's mother and Kamla's mother had gone to town shopping together.

Suddenly there was a ring at the door. 'Oh, that must be Kamla!' cried Kate. 'I told her to call for me after lunch,' and she leapt up from the table.

'Kate! Kate! Manners maketh men *and women*!'

'Yes, Granny!' murmured Kate. 'Please may I leave the table?'

'Yes you may, but don't leap up like that. It's bad for your digestion.'

Kate walked very slowly out of the kitchen, then once out of sight, she flew to the front door and opened it.

Kamla stood there, beaming all over, standing extra tall in her roller skates.

'Are you coming to the park? Bring your skateboard, and we can have races together.'

'Oh yes!' cried Kate excitedly. 'Wait a moment while I get my skateboard.'

'Kate dear!' Kate heard the tone in her grandmother's voice, and sighed. What now?

'Kate dear, I think you should help me clear the table before you rush off and enjoy yourself.'

'But Grandma! Kamla's already here. She's waiting for me,' protested Kate.

'Well, ask Kamla to help you. You know what they say, "Many hands make light work".'

Kate looked at Kamla and shrugged apologetically, but Kamla just sat down on the doorstep and began unlacing her roller skates. 'I don't mind!' she grinned, reassuringly. 'I often have to do it at home.'

To and fro they went, carrying the dishes from the table to the kitchen sink. Grandma put on rubber gloves, ready to do the washing up. At last the table was clear.

'Can we go now?' asked Kate.

'Yes dear, off you go and play. "Make hay while the sun shines!" and thank you, Kamla, for helping. That was very nice of you.'

'That's all right,' answered Kamla.

The two girls hurried to the front door. Kate found her skateboard, while Kamla put on her roller skates again. Finally, they were ready. They opened the door, and then gave a cry of dismay. 'Oh no! It's raining!'

'Good heavens!' gasped Grandma, running up to see. 'You can't possibly go out in that. It's raining cats and dogs!'

'What shall we do?' wailed Kate. They withdrew into the house and shut the door.

'Come, come, dear!' scolded Grandma. 'There must be lots two bright girls like you can do! Why don't you both go and do a jigsaw. I want to settle quietly with a book.' With that, she picked up her Agatha Christie novel and stretched herself out on the settee.

Kamla and Kate stomped upstairs. They went into Kate's bedroom and opened the toy cupboard. They looked at the board games, the jigsaw puzzles, the packs of cards and the dressing-up clothes, but they didn't feel like playing with any of those. They looked at the reading books, the drawing books and the colouring books, but they didn't feel like doing anything like that.

They wandered across the landing to

Kate's parents' bedroom. Facing them was one long, bright mirror over a long, white dressing table. The two girls stood before the mirror and waved at each other. Then Kate pulled a face and Kamla pulled a face and they began laughing and giggling.

Kate looked at all the rows of lipsticks, jars, bottles and tubes of make-up.

'I'm going to make myself up like my mum,' said Kate.

'I'll make myself up like my mum,' said Kamla.

'My mum puts on cream,' said Kate.

'So does mine,' said Kamla.

They opened up a pale blue jar with a gold lid. They dipped their fingers into the fluffy white cream and smeared it all over their faces.

'My mum puts on powder,' said Kate.

'So does mine,' said Kamla.

They opened up a powder box and dabbed their faces with a large soft powder puff. Clouds of powder billowed into the air. They looked at themselves critically in the mirror.

'I think I need some lipstick,' murmured Kate.

'Yes, me too,' agreed Kamla.

They looked at the row of lipsticks lined up like soldiers across the back of the dressing table.

'Which colour shall we choose?' they asked each other.

They began to try them out, dabbing a little from each lipstick on the back of their hands.

'That's too red. That's too pink. That's too orange. That's too glossy,' they commented as they studied each smear.

At last Kate said, 'I'm going to put on a lipstick called Posh Prune.'

And Kamla chose a lipstick called Indian Rose.

'Don't we look beautiful?' they said admiringly as they gazed at their images in the mirror. 'We haven't finished yet though,' said Kate. 'My mum wears mascara when she goes out in the evenings.

'So does mine,' said Kamla.

There was a little black bottle with a

special rounded brush inside. Kate used it first. She leaned right forward towards the mirror, her tongue stuck out between her teeth as she concentrated very hard. Very, very carefully, she brushed the black mascara on to her eyelashes.

When Kamla had done the same, they studied themselves once more in the mirror.

'We look like film stars!' said Kate.

'Something's missing,' said Kamla frowning.

'Red cheeks?' asked Kate, finding another brush to make her cheeks bright.

'No,' murmured Kate.

'Eye shadow?' asked Kate, finding another palette of colours with a brush, and painting her eyelids purple.

'No,' Kamla shook her head. Then she said, 'I know what's missing. Bindi!'

'Bindi?' exclaimed Kate. 'What's that?'

'That's the red spot Indian ladies wear in the middle of their foreheads,' explained Kamla. 'My mum has a little row of pots with different shades of bindi.'

Kate looked on her mother's dressing table. 'My mum doesn't wear that,' she said.

'I won't be properly made up if I don't wear a bindi,' announced Kamla. 'I'll just have to use lipstick.'

She took the lipstick marked Indian Rose and pressed the tip to her forehead. It came out a bit big and a bit blotchy, but Kamla looked satisfied. 'That's better,' she said.

'I think I'll put that on too,' said Kate.

Kamla laughed. 'You'll look funny!' she cried.

'I don't care,' insisted Kate. 'I like it.'

Once more the two girls stood side by side staring at each other in front of the long mirror. 'Do we look like grown-up ladies?' they asked themselves.

Then Kamla said, 'I'm going to try and coil my hair into a bun like my mother does.'

'Let me do it for you,' cried Kate. She loved brushing out Kamla's long, black hair. It was so long, it nearly touched her bottom. Kamla liked having her hair brushed. It was so soothing that she often went into a daydream.

'I wish my hair was as long as yours,' murmured Kate.

'I wish I could have my hair cut like yours,' said Kamla. 'Mum would let me, but Dad says he likes Indian ladies to have long hair.'

Kate looked at her fair hair which fell to her shoulders, and tossed it.

'If mine was a little longer, and yours was a little shorter, we'd be the same.'

'Hmm,' agreed Kamla.

'I could cut it for you,' suggested Kate.

'I know where Mum keeps the scissors.'

'I don't know,' said Kamla doubtfully. 'I might get into trouble.'

'Oh go on, Kamla, let me!' cried Kate. She was longing to play at being a hairdresser. 'I'll only cut off a little bit. No one will notice.'

'Oh OK,' replied Kamla. 'If you let me do your hair afterwards.'

Kate agreed. She went to the bathroom and opened the cupboard door. There inside, with the tweezers and shaving things and the first aid kit and the cotton wool, was a pair of long, sharp, scissors. Even as she looked at them, a little voice in her head said, 'Oh, Kate. Do you think you should?' But Kate didn't take any notice of the little voice. She grabbed the scissors and snapped them in the air. She liked the sound. Snip, snip!'

Kamla looked at the scissors anxiously. 'Only a very little,' she reminded Kate.

'I promise,' promised Kate.

Snip, snap, snip, snap! Kate tried to cut in a straight line across the bottom.

Whoops! It went a bit crooked. She

78

snipped again to try and straighten it, but then another bit went crooked. She didn't say anything to Kamla, but went on snipping and snapping trying to straighten the bottom of Kamla's hair.

'Is it looking all right?' asked Kamla turning round suspiciously.

'Don't turn round!' cried Kate. 'You'll make me go crooked.'

'Don't cut off too much!' begged Kamla.

'I'm not,' protested Kate, but, whoops, she cut another zigzag into Kamla's hair,

and Kate went on snipping and snipping to get it straight. Soon there was a big pile of black hair on the carpet. Kamla looked down and gasped with horror. She jumped up.

'Stop, stop, stop!' she wailed. 'Is all that my hair?' She twisted round trying to see in the mirror. 'Look! You've cut it so short it's nearly to the middle of my back!'

'It looks shorter because you're twisting round,' retorted Kate. 'It's not that short. Anyway, it's your turn now. You can cut off some of my hair, but only a little!'

Snip snap snip! Kamla tried to trim Kate's hair.

Whoops! It went a bit crooked. She didn't say anything to Kate, but went on snipping and snapping to get it straight. Soon there was a big pile of yellow hair on the carpet. Every time she cut one bit straight, it seemed to make another bit crooked.

'Is it looking all right?' asked Kate trying to twist her head over her shoulder.

'Don't turn round!' cried Kamla. 'Oh look what you've made me do!'

'What have you done?' wailed Kate jumping up. She put her hand up her back to feel the ends of her hair. Then she saw the pile of yellow hair on the carpet.

'Oh no!' she groaned. 'I must be nearly bald.'

Suddenly they heard the front door open. Kate's mum called up the stairs. 'Hello, Kate, I'm back!'

Kamla's mum called up the stairs. 'Hello, Kamla, I'm back!'

Kamla and Kate looked at each other and couldn't say a word. They heard footsteps coming up the stairs. It was Grandma. 'Kamla, Kate!' she called out. 'Your mothers are home.'

'We're coming!' Kate managed to squeak.

They listened. The footsteps went back down the stairs.

Kate heard her mum say, 'They seem rather quiet up there.'

Kamla heard her mum say, 'What have they been up to?'

'I told them to do a jigsaw,' said Grandma.

'Kate! Kamla! Come downstairs. We want to see you,' cried the two mothers.

Kamla and Kate didn't move.

They heard one pair of footsteps coming up the stairs. 'Oh, no!' cried Kamla's mother.

They heard a second pair of footsteps coming up the stairs. 'Oh, no!' cried Kate's mother.

They heard a third pair of footsteps coming up the stairs. 'Oh, no!' cried Grandma.

They looked at the opened jars of cream, the toppled-over lipsticks, the mascara brush and the cheek blusher brush, and the two piles of hair on the floor; one pile black as night, and the other pile yellow as buttercups.

'Oh no!' They all cried.

'We didn't know what else to play,' whimpered Kate.

'We didn't feel like doing jigsaws,' stammered Kamla.

'Well you know what they say, don't you?' murmured Grandmother knowingly.

82

Everyone looked at her.
' "The devil finds work for idle hands." '

7

The Bridegroom Gets a Pasting

It was Saturday. Kamla came rushing round early to Kate's house.

'Quick! Come on! We're all invited!'

'Where?' cried Kate. 'Invited where?'

'Over to Naresh. He's marrying Muni today, and they're starting the pasting ceremony. Come on, now. I don't want to miss it!'

'The pasting ceremony? What's that?' asked Kate.

But Kamla wouldn't take the time to answer. 'You'll see,' she gasped, as she tugged Kate's arm.

Kate's mum and dad said they would follow in a minute, so Kamla and Kate raced off down the street and round the corner to Naresh's house.

'Oh look!' Kate exclaimed with wonder. The ordinary little semi-detached house was transformed into a palace. Garlands of flowers were hung from window to window and all round the front door, and the garden path had been decorated, using different coloured chalks to make patterns all the way up.

All sorts of people streamed in and out. Ancient white-haired grandfathers held the hands of timid toddlers, while older children feverishly weaved their way through the crowd.

The front door was wide open. Kate could see right through the house to the back garden. Flags fluttered along the fences and balloons hung from the apple trees. 'I wonder if my wedding day will be like this,' murmured Kate.

Kamla and Kate walked through into the kitchen. Something mysterious was going on. Naresh's mother, grandmother and older sisters were bent over a large bucket. Each had a stick and was stirring. One would add yellow powder and another would tip some water, and they

all stirred till they had a thick paste. There was the rich spicy smell of an Indian restaurant.

'Are they going to make a curry?' asked Kate.

'You'll see,' grinned Kamla teasingly.

Suddenly, the stirring stopped. Mother, grandmother and older sisters straightened up.

'All right then, it's ready,' they said. 'Where's Naresh?' They had mischievous smiles on their faces.

'Where's Naresh?' The call rang out through the house and into the back garden.

Everyone looked around. 'Naresh! Naresh! Has anyone seen Naresh?'

'He must be hiding,' someone cried.

'Let's find him then,' yelled another.

'Why is Naresh hiding?' asked Kate, puzzled.

'You'll see, you'll see!' Kamla hugged herself with delight. 'Come on! Let's hunt for him.'

Everyone was searching. Upstairs and downstairs they went, peering in cupboards, checking under the beds, throwing back curtains, pushing aside chairs and sofas, and they even looked in the laundry basket! But Naresh was nowhere to be found.

Kamla and Kate went out into the garden. 'Let's see if he's hiding in the shed,' suggested Kamla. But though they looked in the shed, on top of the shed and behind the shed, there was still no sign of him.

'What are they going to do to him when they find him?' asked Kate with concern.

'You'll see, you'll see!' repeated Kamla. She wasn't giving anything away.

Then suddenly, Kate saw a slight movement out of the corner of her eye. A branch quivered near the top of the apple tree. She opened her mouth to shout out, then shut it again. She wandered slowly over and looked up. There was Naresh, perched right up at the top of the tree. He looked at her silently pleading. He put a finger to his lips, then pressed both hands together as in prayer, beseeching her not to give him away. Kate ran back to Kamla and grabbed her arm. 'Come on, Kamla! Let's look indoors again.'

But another pair of sharp eyes had noticed the branch shake in the apple tree. A small child shook herself loose from her grandfather's hand, and tottered over to stand underneath. She began to point and jump up and down. 'I found him! I found him!' she gurgled.

At first no one took any notice of the little girl as they rushed here, there and everywhere. Then the child trundled back to her grandfather and began to tug him and tug him.

'Come Chachaji! Come!' She dragged him over to the apple tree and pointed.

'Naresh!' She exclaimed proudly.

Naresh had been found! The word spread like wildfire. Everyone came running and surrounded the apple tree. Kate came too with Kamla. She looked up at Naresh, still perched on the branch at the top, and she shrugged as if to say, 'It wasn't my fault they found you. I didn't give you away.'

Naresh just shrugged back and smiled.

Then suddenly, the crowd made way. Naresh's sisters pushed through, carrying the bucket of yellow paste. Excited expectation rippled through everyone.

'Come on down, Naresh!' advised a voice sternly, but with laughter.

'Come down, come down!' cried others.

But Naresh tightened his hold and

wouldn't come down. 'If you want me, you'll have to come and get me,' he taunted.

Two of his friends leapt up on to the tree and began to climb. Up and up they went. Soon they were within arm's reach of his dangling legs. They poked and prodded at him. 'Come on down, you can't escape!'

Naresh's sisters held up the bucket. One of his friends bent down and scooped up a fistful of yellow paste and hurled it at Naresh. A great shout of delight went up, as the paste hit him full in the chest.

Naresh looked at his friends climbing closer and closer. He looked at the people below and he looked at the bucket of yellow paste. 'Ah well,' he said with a sigh, 'I know when I'm beaten.' Just as one of his friends was about to hurl another fist full of paste at him, he swung down on the branch and dropped to the ground.

With a roar of triumph, everyone jumped on him. They pulled off his shirt, his pullover, his trousers, his shoes and his socks, and began smearing the yellow paste all over his body; over his arms and legs and back and face, and even all over his head and hair.

Kate gazed in horror. 'Poor Naresh!' she wailed. 'Why are they doing this to him?'

'That's what they do to bridegrooms in India!' chuckled Kamla. 'It means he'll have to have a really good bath and scrub to get clean for his wedding! Come on! Let's join in too!'

Kate paused, but only for two seconds. 'Yes!' she cried with glee. 'Let's!'

They both rushed at the bucket. They plunged their arms in and clutched handfuls of paste.

'Not you too!' wailed Naresh, pretending to be distressed, as Kamla and Kate slapped paste all over his back. 'I thought you were my friends!'

At last all the paste in the bucket was finished. Naresh stood there dripping like a blob of melting butter. He was covered in yellow paste from head to toe.

'Now to get you clean!' called a voice. A young man held a hosepipe and pointed it

at Naresh. 'Turn on the water!' he shouted.

A jet of silver water arched through the air and spurted all over the poor bridegroom. Everyone scattered.

Suddenly Kate noticed her mum and dad watching the scene from a safe distance with Kamla's mum and dad. The girls rushed over.

'Did you see what they did to Naresh!' cried Kate.

'That's what happened to me on my wedding day,' murmured Kamla's dad.

'It's enough to put you off getting married,' remarked Kate's dad with a shudder.

'What did you do before your wedding then?' Kate asked her father.

'I'll tell you what he did,' retorted Kate's mother. 'He went off with all his men friends and had a stag party. They ate and drank and fooled about all night, and your father nearly didn't wake up in time for his wedding. I should have turned the hosepipe on to him!'

'What about the brides? Don't they have any fun?' asked Kate.

'Oh, Muni is having a party too with her friends,' said Kamla. 'They'll be joking and teasing her, but it won't be rough.'

'Sounds like the kind of party I had with my friends,' Kate's mum remembered.

'Look at Naresh!' cried Kamla. 'He's all nice and clean now.'

Naresh stood there like a prince, his body glistening in the sunlight, while his mother, grandmother and sisters rubbed him all over with oil.

'Now he's ready to go and put on his wedding clothes,' said Kamla's mum.

'Can we go now and put on our wedding clothes?' asked Kate excitedly. 'I've got a lovely new dress. We bought it yesterday. It's blue, with puffed sleeves and a lovely twirly skirt.

'Oh yes! I want to get into my new clothes,' cried Kamla. 'I've got a brand new set of kurta pyjama. They were specially made for me by my aunt. They're pink silk with green and gold borders, and a lovely pink and gold threaded veil to go with it.'

'Get into your wedding clothes?' exclaimed Kate's dad incredulously. 'Goodness gracious, you two, have you seen yourselves?'

Kamla looked at Kate. Kate looked at Kamla. They hadn't stopped to look at each other before. They got a shock! Kate had yellow smears all up her arms, and smudges on her cheeks and yellow splatters in her hair. Kamla had streaks on her forehead and stripes down her legs and lumps of paste clogged in her plaits.

'You know what you two need before you get into your clothes for the wedding?' Kamla's dad wagged a finger at them.

The two girls looked at each other and laughed. 'What we need is a really good bath!'